First published in Great Britain 2013 by Walker Books Ltd, 87 Vauxhall Walk, London SE11 5HJ • 1 2 3 4 5 6 7 8 9 10
© 2010 Taro Miura • English language translation © 2013 Walker Books Ltd • First published in Japan in 2010
as *Chiisana Ôsama* by Kaisei-sha Publishing Co., Ltd, Tokyo • English translation rights arranged
with Kaisei-sha Publishing Co., Ltd through Japan Foreign-Rights Centre • The right of Taro Miura to
be identified as author and illustrator of this work has been asserted by him in accordance with
the Copyright, Designs and Patents Act 1988 • This book has been typeset in Burbank Medium
Printed in China • All rights reserved • No part of this book may be reproduced, transmitted or stored in an
information retrieval system in any form or by any means, graphic, electronic or mechanical, including
photocopying, taping and recording, without prior written permission from the publisher • British Library
Cataloguing in Publication Data: a catalogue record for this book is available from the British Library.
ISBN 978-1-4063-4819-4 • www.walker.co.uk

WALKER BOOKS

AND SUBSIDIARIES

LONDON • BOSTON • SYDNEY • AUCKLAND

The Tiny King

Taro Miura

Once upon a time, in a land far, far away,
there was a Tiny King.

y king lived all alone in a big, big castle.

He had an army of big soldiers with long spears
and stern faces. Wherever the Tiny King went,
the soldiers marched behind.
Left, right, left, right, left, right.

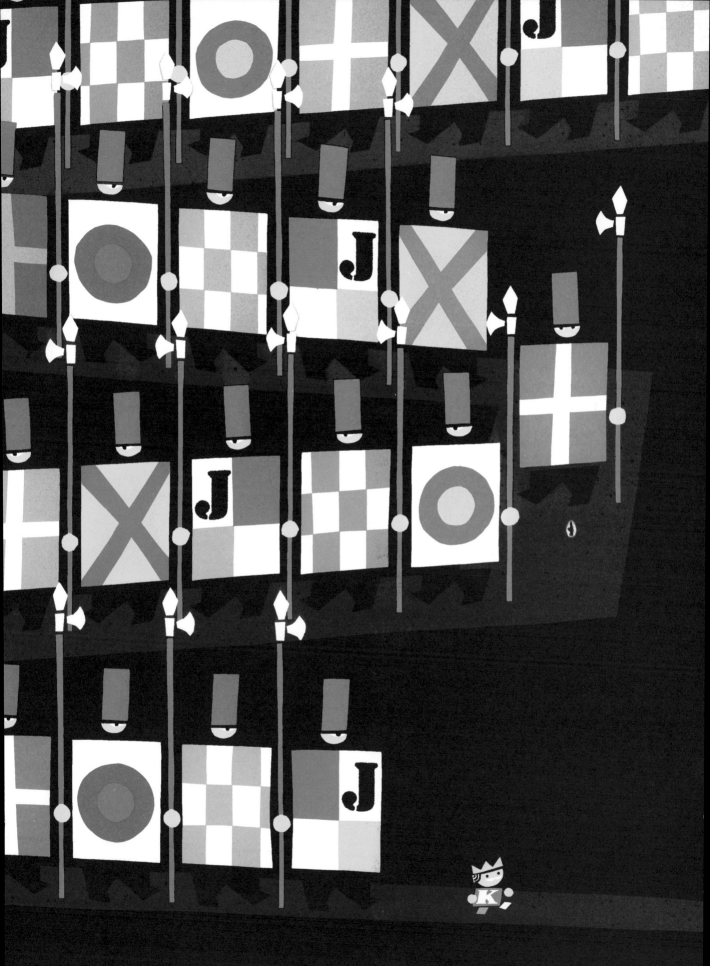

He could never finish so much food all by himself.

The Tiny King had a big white horse.

But he was so tiny and the horse was so big
that he fell off every time he tried to ride.

The Tiny King had a big, big bathtub.
It even had a water fountain.

The Tiny King's bed was a big, big bed.
But he slept in it all alone every night.

The Tiny King was so sad and so lonely
that he never slept very well.

Then one day,
the Tiny King fell in love with
a Big Princess and asked her
if she would be his Queen.

She said yes!

And soon they were
happily married.

Not long after, the Tiny King and the Big Queen were blessed with children—lots of children.

The Tiny King was so happy that he sent
his army of soldiers home on holiday.
They all marched off—left, right, left, right—
back to their families.

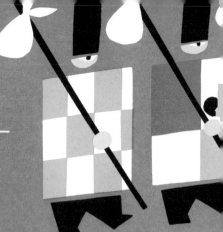

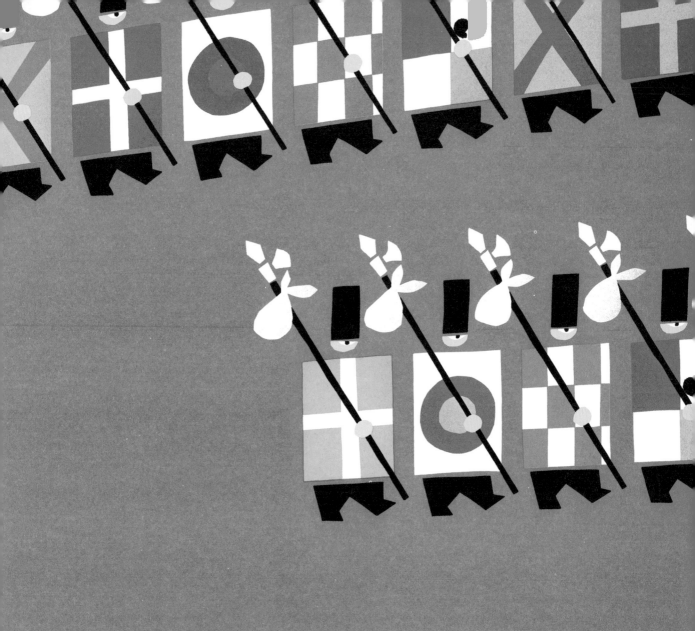

Now the Tiny King's castle no longer felt so big.
The children ran around, laughing and playing
all day long.

The Tiny King and his family gathered round the big table every day.

Together, they had no trouble finishing the enormous feast of delicious food.

And look! The big white horse pulled the Tiny King and the Big Queen in a carriage while the children rode on his back.

Here they are, on their way to a picnic.

Now bath time was a real riot!
The Tiny King and his family splished
and splashed together every day.

And what about the Tiny King's big, big bed,
where he had been so sad and so lonely?

Well, when everyone snuggled up side by side,
it was just the right size.

And the Tiny King slept soundly at last.
Look, here he is, fast asleep.

Good night, Tiny King.